Love without Words

Molly O'Malley Pitman
Illustrated by Jeffrey Scott Perdziak

Kevin W W Blackley Books, LLC
Copyrighted Material
Love without Words

For information about this title or to order other books and/or electronic media, contact the publisher:
Kevin W W Blackley Books, LLC
Buffalo, NY 14215
www.kevinblackley.com
books@kwwilson.com

For more information about the author, visit:
www.sweetcharlottes.org
sweetcharlottes@yahoo.com

Author photograph by Kristin La Driere Family Photography
Cover artwork inspired by a photograph from Elizabeth Snyder Photography, LLC
Artwork by Jeffrey Scott Perdziak

Library of Congress Control Number:
2016901683

ISBN:
978-0-9960839-3-5 Hardcover

Printed in the United States of America

"The greatest thing you'll ever learn is to love and be loved in return."

—eden ahbez, 1947

*This special heart was created with love
by Charlotte Pitman.*

A hug and a smile, a cuddle or kiss,

Wonderful ways to say "I LOVE YOU"—
We all know this.

But if you open your eyes wider than wide,
You may find a surprise:
There's even more love inside.

It's a feeling you share,
It's not always heard,

But you can LOVE and BE LOVED,
Without a single word.

Have you ever shared a yummy treat on that first summer day?
A quiet celebration of the fun on its way!

A day at the park with family and friends,
The thrill of the slide that just doesn't end!

9

Maybe your best friend has no words at all,
Yet is by your side in winter, spring, summer, and fall.

A day-trip with Grandma to someplace that's new,
A day of adventure—exploring too!

Just hanging out, when time stands still,
Hoping patiently there may be a thrill.

What about a smile that really says it all?
A smile can make a difference, BIG and small.

Taking a walk is a nice thing to do,
Enjoying a moment that's meant only for you.

Nature is best when it's shared with another:
The sights and the sounds and the love from your brother.

21

Making the silliest faces you've got,
Love can be silly, so really, why not?

Relaxing and cuddling on a lazy day,
Letting anything that troubles you fade away.

Memories are made in the sun, in the sand,
Splashing in water—vacations are grand!

Do you get excited when holidays are near?
Trick-or-treating's fun with the friends you hold dear.

29

Creating a gift with a talent that's yours,
Giving, like receiving, will open love's doors.

Love is sharing; it means, "Please come join me.
You're special to me and I'd like you to see."

Another day at the playground ... 1, 2, 3!
Making memories that last a lifetime, just he and she.

Moments and memories show a love that is true,
They are beautiful ways to say, "I love you!"

If there's one thing I know to be certain and real,
You are SPECIAL,
You are LOVED,
And so ... LOVED YOU SHOULD FEEL!

About the Author and Her Inspiration

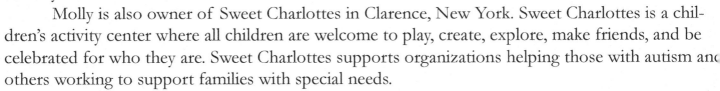

Molly O'Malley Pitman is mother to son Donovan and daughter Charlotte. Donovan, now twelve, has autism and was nonverbal until the age of almost six. Inspired by their relationship as young children when Charlotte questioned why her brother would not reciprocate when she said to him, "I love you," Molly responded by emphasizing that love can be an action and not only a word.

The illustrations in this book are a collection of moments and memories that took place in their younger childhood. The author hopes that others might have similar experiences and be able to identify and celebrate such love in their own lives.

Molly is also owner of Sweet Charlottes in Clarence, New York. Sweet Charlottes is a children's activity center where all children are welcome to play, create, explore, make friends, and be celebrated for who they are. Sweet Charlottes supports organizations helping those with autism and others working to support families with special needs.

The author invites you to visit her website, http://www.sweetcharlottes.org/.

♥

I dedicate *Love without Words* to my brother Jay, who demonstrated his unconditional love until his passing in November of 2012. For some time, he too struggled to "use his words," yet constantly said "I love you" with his bright blue eyes and unforgettable smile. He always prayed that Donovan would find his voice, and I believe he had a part in our miracle. Donovan deeply loved him, as do all of us. Your legacy will live on, Jay. We will continue to love.

About the Illustrator

Jeffrey Scott Perdziak has always been an artist. Ever since he can remember, he's been creating reality on paper with his pencils. Jeff has completed many different projects. He has illustrated everything from pencil portraits to a life-sized painting of a train on the side of a bowling alley, namely the West Shore Railroad mural in Clarence, NY.

You'll find some of his wildlife artwork with a wildlife rehabilitation group called AWARE. His artwork is also printed on T-shirts and sold to raise money for the group.

The artist designs T-shirts, too. He has designed for music artists such as BB King, the Rolling Stones, Jason Aldean, and Carrie Underwood.

Jeff is a big comic book fan. He's working on his own comic book creation, *The Menagerie*, with the Visions Comic Art Group in Buffalo, NY, doing the writing and the artwork. Even though he has created his own characters, his favorite of all is Superman. *Love without Words* is the fourth children's book he has illustrated. He is also the illustrator of the Mubu the Morph series.

He says, "*Love without Words* was a perfect fit for me. I love being able to share my art with others—especially when it has such a wonderful message."

CPSIA information can be obtained
at www.ICGtesting.com
Printed in the USA
BVOW05*1244060217
475386BV00002B/2/P